For Milly and Palace, Leisa and Jane, we love you!
A & S

First published in Great Britain in 2005
by Orion Children's Books
a division of the Orion Publishing Group Ltd
Orion House
5 Upper St Martin's Lane
London WC2H 9EA

Text and illustrations copyright © Selina Young 2005

Design by Sarah Hodder

The right of Selina Young to be identified as the
author and illustrator of this work has been asserted.

A catalogue record for this book is available from
the British Library
Printed and bound in Italy
ISBN 1 84255 118 3

www.orionbooks.co.uk

Oh, have we
started?
I need to
be on the
next
page!

All About Me

A hundred things that happened to me between 0 and 3

Selina Young

Orion
Children's Books

Hello, I'm Alfred Sage. This is my lion, Snuffy, and my cat, Nero. And this book is all about me.

Goodness me, what a lot of fuss about something so small!

When I was just new I was really little.
I had tiny fingers and tiny toes.

I slept in a flax basket.

When I was hungry I CRIED.

I drank lots of milk.

I love milk.

Daddy said I was sometimes sick on his shoulder.

I wriggled a lot when it was time to change
my nappy.

I used lots of nappies, sometimes eight a day.

I could grab.

Mum doesn't like that!

Kicking off my socks was great ...

whoops!

... so was splashing in my baby bath.

Mum likes that.

I was five weeks old when I smiled for the first time.

At five months I could sit up ...

Just as well that cushion was there.

... nearly.

Bouncing in my jolly jumper was fun.

B o u n c e

B o u n c e

B o u n c e

Go to sleep, Alfie!

Sometimes I woke up in the middle of the night.

He can't be hungry already.

Look at all these things I put in my mouth!

Mum gave me a teething ring when my teeth hurt.

My first food was mashed up carrots and peas, but I didn't like it.

kiwi fruit

apples

melon

avocados

corn

potatoes

broccoli

Not sure I like that!

I chatted to my toys.

Soon I grew so much I didn't fit in my baby bath.
Mum put me in the real bath.

I could brush my hair with my nice, soft baby brush.

Look, I'm crawling.

Mum put up a gate

so I wouldn't fall

down the stairs.

I was just the right height
for Grandma's dog to lick me.

I only liked
Mummy kissing me.

I could eat bananas all by myself.

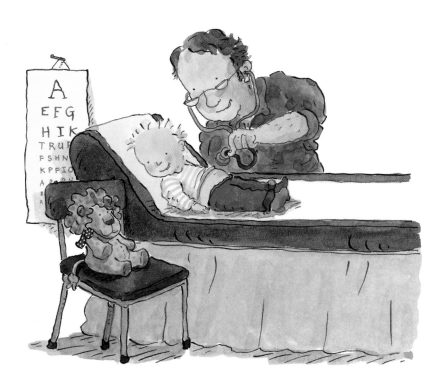

This is me at the clinic for my health check.
I was very healthy!

Standing up took lots of practice.

Soon I could stand up without holding on to anything.

When I was one Mum made me a big cake with a candle on top.

I had lots of presents. I liked the wrapping paper best!

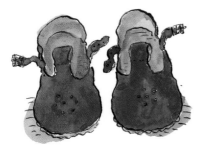

my first shoes

When I started to walk Mum said I needed shoes. They felt funny.

Glad I don't need to wear shoes.

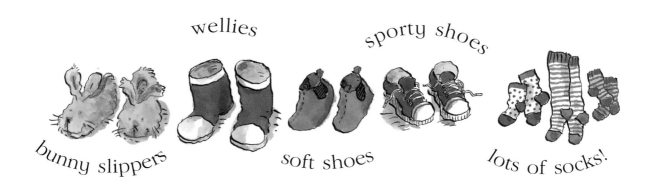

bunny slippers

wellies

soft shoes

sporty shoes

lots of socks!

I was good
at climbing ...

... but coming
downstairs
was tricky.

My first word was 'ball'.

Soon I knew lots of words. I could shout very loudly.

I loved books.

With all my new teeth, I needed a toothbrush
and my own toothpaste.

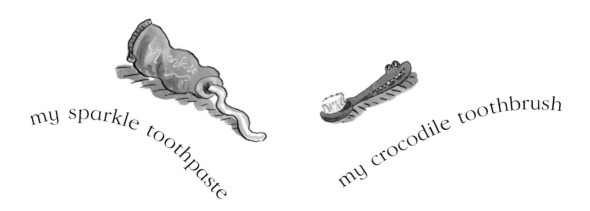

my sparkle toothpaste

my crocodile toothbrush

I didn't like my hair being washed.

Silly Alfie, it's a potty!

Why did I think that was a hat?

Crayons worked well on the wall.

Look how fast I raced on my ladybird.

I liked gardening.

I liked painting ...

... and playing Daddy's guitar.

When I was quite big I had a new bed,

and new space
rocket jammys.

I loved my blankie and I cried
when I couldn't find it.

I liked bedtime
stories.

Once upon a time
there was a huge
stripy tent. Inside
lived a pretty little
spotty pony called...
Sparky!

this is a magical tale.

Oh, that's what a potty is for.

Now I get to wear pull-ups.

I grew out of all my baby clothes.

Look how tall I am.

Mum asked some of my friends to my second birthday party. I had a huge cake and lots of presents.

bendy snake
from Lily

bubble blower
from Palace

train from Jack

JUNGLE
JANGLE
sticker fun

sticker book
from Rylie

Yum!

colour pencils and pencil
sharpener from Milly

rainbow torch
from Louie

Tea
time!

Don't want my hair brushed.

Don't think I'd like that either!

But WHY Mummy?

Because Mummy says, Alfie.

Sometimes I didn't like sharing.

Sometimes I did.

I liked getting up early.

I wear boxers now

checky ones

spotty ones

stripy ones

very smart!

and I can use the big toilet!

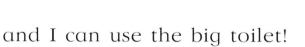

My new trike went really fast.

That's me going swimming in my new trunks and blow-up armbands.

I liked trying lots of different food.
Spaghetti was fun.

I liked strawberries best.

These eggs seemed
harder on our picnic.

I liked playing in the park.
I liked the roundabout best.

I could get dressed all by myself.

I liked dressing up – clip, clop –

and colouring in.

I had a new car seat for driving everywhere. I helped Mum with the shopping, and if I was good, she took me to the café.

Isn't Alfie being good waiting for Mum to get our treat.

I am three today. I'm having a fancy dress party.
My chocolate caterpillar birthday cake looks yummy.

Aargh, I've had a bad dream.

I loved my blankie so much it fell to pieces,
but Grandma made me a new one.

I like the flower.

Grandma, I've got Chicken's Pops.

The Doctor gave Mum some pink lotion
to stop my spots itching.

Watch out! Here I come!

GOAL!

I love playing in my sandpit with my best friends.
We are making volcanoes.

I like watching videos. I like Peter Pan.

Lily

Mia

Palace

Monty

I have lots of friends at playgroup.

Milly

Rylie

Me!

Betsy

Jack

I get glitter gel when I have my hair cut.

Do you think my tail needs a trim?

Look at my new sunnies.

I love to help Mummy with the jobs ...

... and to have my friends round for tea.

My toys are amazing.

Let's dress up.

Mum says I can choose a pet.
I want a guinea pig called Barry.

My new raincoat and umbrella
are just right for rainy days.

I can count.

I like playing pirates with Grandma.

I can button up my jammys all by myself.

Sometimes I'm good for the babysitter,
and sometimes I'm not.

Story time.

Wow! Look how tall I am now.

I can write my name.

I love your hugs, Mum.

I love you, Mum.

I love you too, Alfie.

The End

Bye!